This book belongs to:

_____

5-MINUTE ADVENTURE STORIES

Written by
Laura Driscoll
and **Sarah Heller**

Illustrated by
**The Disney
Storybook Artists**
and **Ken Becker**

Contents

Buzz to the Rescue!

"There you go, pardners," Andy said as he packed Sheriff Woody, Jessie the cowgirl, and Bullseye the horse into his backpack. Jessie couldn't wait to go to cowboy camp—Woody said there were *real* horses there.

"Almost ready?" Andy's mom asked as she poked her head into his room. Glancing at Andy's half-open backpack, she shook her head. "Andy, you know the rules. Just one toy."

"Oh, all right," Andy said with a sigh. "Sorry, guys." He lifted Jessie and

Bullseye out of the bag and placed them on the windowsill.

Jessie and Bullseye watched out the window as Andy walked to the car. Jessie swallowed hard to keep from crying as the car drove away.

Bullseye nuzzled her shoulder, and Jessie patted him on the head. "I know you're disappointed, too," she said sadly.

Bullseye whinnied as Jessie climbed down from the window and flopped into a box full of books. Andy's mom had just put the box in his room that morning, and Jessie thought its high sides would make for a nice, private place. No such luck. She had only been there a moment when Buzz Lightyear, a Space Ranger toy, poked his head over the side of the box.

"Don't be sad, Jessie," Buzz said, climbing into the box. "You don't need to go to camp to have an adventure. We can have a great time here. Right, guys?"

All of Andy's toys agreed. Rex the dinosaur, Hamm the piggy bank, and Slinky Dog gathered around the box to cheer Jessie up.

"Thank you all," Jessie told her friends, "but I think I'd just like to be alone for a little while."

The toys nodded sadly and left.

Suddenly, a Green Army Man yelled, "Red alert!"

Someone was coming. All of the toys fell lifeless to the floor as Andy's doorknob turned and the babysitter walked in.

"I'll be down in a minute, Molly!" the babysitter yelled to Andy's little sister.

She looked down at a list in her hand. "Let's see. . . . 'Put box of old books in attic,'" she read.

Old books? Jessie thought. Oh, no! While the babysitter peered at her list, Jesse glanced down at the side of the box. It read: OLD BOOKS.

Jessie was about to be put into storage in the attic!

Jessie lay perfectly still as the babysitter turned out the light and closed the attic door. Then she climbed out of the box. "Let me out of here!" she cried.

Jessie pushed and banged on the attic door. It would not budge. Looking around the attic, Jessie spotted a small window. She climbed up on a few boxes so she could look out.

The view was the same as the one from Andy's window—only higher. Jessie realized that Andy's room must be directly below. Suddenly, Jessie had an idea.

Meanwhile, the toys in Andy's room were planning a rescue.

"Okay, recruits, here's the plan," Buzz said as he pointed to Etch a Sketch, who quickly drew a picture of the stairs to the attic.

"The Green Army Men will lead the attack and radio back if they run into danger. At the top of the stairs, the men will form a pyramid and

grab on to the doorknob, opening the door," Buzz said. Etch a Sketch drew quickly to keep up with Buzz's words. "Once the door is open, I'll go in and get Jessie," Buzz added.

The toys nodded. They all knew what to do.

"Let's go, everyone!" Buzz cried. "We've got a toy to save!"

Jessie managed to open an old trunk in the attic, and she began digging around inside. There were some old newspapers, three books, a baby blanket, and a jump rope.

A jump rope! Jessie pulled the jump rope out of the trunk and tied it into a quick slipknot.

It's not the best lasso I've ever seen, she said to herself, but it'll have to do for now.

Jessie twirled the makeshift lasso a few times and threw the loop over the window lock. Then she hauled herself up onto the ledge. She opened the window a few inches and crawled outside.

Don't look down, she told herself as she stepped onto the ledge.

Just then, Jessie heard someone fiddling with the attic doorknob. Oh, no, Jessie thought. The babysitter is back! Jessie closed her eyes, grabbed the rope, and jumped.

"Green Army Men, fall in!" Sarge commanded.

The sergeant gave Buzz a snappy salute, then turned to his men and barked a few commands. Within moments, they had formed a pyramid.

Buzz held his breath as the Green Army Man at the top grabbed the knob. He fumbled with it, but after a moment it turned! The door was open.

"Hang on, Jessie!" Buzz cried as he ran into the attic. "We'll rescue you!"

But Jessie was nowhere to be seen!

Buzz gasped as he looked around and spotted the open window. Scrambling up some old cardboard boxes, Buzz hauled himself out onto the ledge. Down below, he saw Jessie. She was dangling at the end of a jump rope—it looked as if she were about to fall!

"Don't let go, Jessie!" Buzz shouted. "I'm coming for you!"

Buzz deployed his wings. Then, taking a deep breath, he dove out the window.

Jessie looked up and saw Buzz falling out the attic window—right toward her.

"Look out!" Buzz cried.

Thinking fast, Jessie swung her legs out and caught Buzz just as he was about to fall past her. He was heavy, and the rope jerked under his weight.

"Whoa!" Jessie shouted as she and Buzz swung forward—right through Andy's open window. Hearing the noise, all of Andy's toys ran into the room, to find Buzz and Jessie lying on the floor.

"Are you okay?" Rex asked.

Buzz was the first to sit up. "I'm more than okay!" he crowed. "Our rescue effort was successful, everyone! We saved Jessie!"

Jessie laughed and stood up. "Is that where you all were—rescuing me? Well, thanks,

everybody!" Jessie grinned as she looked around at her good friends. "Even though I didn't get to go to cowboy camp, this has been the best adventure ever! Yee-hah!"

"Yee-hah!" all the toys cheered, welcoming Jessie back to where she belonged.

101 DALMATIANS

Puppy Trouble

"**W**e won't be gone long," Pongo promised Perdita. The Dalmatians were joining their human pets, Roger and Anita, for a picnic with old friends. It was a beautiful summer day, and Pongo was excited to get to the park.

"I'm just not sure we should leave the puppies," Perdita said. "Will Nanny be able to handle all fifteen of them by herself?"

Pongo smiled at his little Dalmatians. They were curled up snugly together in their sleeping basket.

"What could possibly go wrong?" he asked Perdita. "The puppies are napping. Besides, Nanny can handle anything."

Perdita nodded, trying to forget her worries as she followed Pongo into the sunshine. Pongo is right, she told herself firmly—the puppies will be absolutely fine.

It was not long before the puppies started to yawn and stretch. Rolly's paw hit Lucky in the ear, waking him.

The smell of fresh summer air made Lucky want to go outside. "Let's get Nanny to take us for a walk!" Lucky urged the other puppies.

When Nanny finished watering the plants, she turned and saw fifteen puppies eagerly holding their leashes in their mouths. "Oh, dear," she said, looking into their big, hopeful eyes. "Well, I suppose puppies do need to go for a walk now and then."

With seven leashes in her right hand and eight in her left, Nanny followed the puppies onto the sidewalks of London. Lucky strained against his leash as they neared the playground. He couldn't wait to play on the slide!

When they reached the park, Nanny unhooked their leashes and breathed a sigh of relief as the puppies scampered off. The puppies had a wonderful time at the playground. Patch and Pepper loved digging in the sandbox. Rolly found a rope to chew.

Lucky spotted a pretty butterfly. He got ready to pounce, but the butterfly flew up high and landed on the steps to a slide. Lucky chased the butterfly up the steps, all the way to the top.

The butterfly landed on a nearby wall. Lucky jumped from the top of the slide and landed next to the butterfly, but it flew away again. "Look at me!" Lucky barked happily. "I'm taller than everyone else!"

But his brothers and sisters didn't hear him. They were busy playing. They were so busy, in fact, that they didn't see Lucky jump from the top of the wall to chase the butterfly and disappear to the other side.

When Lucky jumped off the wall, he didn't land on the ground. Instead, he landed in the back of a fire truck. It started speeding down the road.

Whee-oo! Whee-oo! The sirens blared.

Woof! Woof! Lucky barked. "I'm a fire dog!"

Lucky enjoyed his ride, but he was glad when the truck pulled to a stop. He knew he had to get back to the playground.

The firemen were busy getting the ladder from the back of the truck. They ran to a big tree.

Meow! Lucky saw that there was a kitten stuck in the tree. He watched one of the firemen climb up the tall ladder, then he jumped off the truck.

"A puppy!" someone said with a squeal. Lucky looked up and saw a little girl with curly red hair, pushing a doll carriage. She reached down and picked him up.

"You can be my new dolly," the little girl said as she tied a bonnet around Lucky's head and dropped him into the carriage. "I'm going to keep you forever."

Lucky shook his head as hard as he could, but the bonnet would not come off. *Grrr*, Lucky growled. He did not like being treated like a doll. Besides, he had to get back to his family!

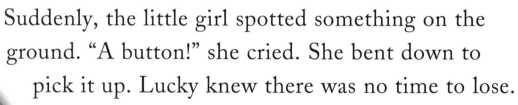

Suddenly, the little girl spotted something on the ground. "A button!" she cried. She bent down to pick it up. Lucky knew there was no time to lose. He jumped out of the carriage and pawed off the bonnet. Then he ran down the street as fast as he could.

At the end of the block, Lucky cocked his ears and listened. He could hear barking! His brothers and sisters were only a couple blocks away.

Lucky raced across the street. He heard a horn honking as a car swerved to avoid him, driving into a mud puddle. Dirty water splashed all over Lucky,

but he ran on and on. When he finally made it to the playground, he was out of breath.

Inside the playground, Nanny was trying to count the puppies, but they kept running around.

"Oh, I give up!" she said finally.

Woof! Woof! Lucky barked as he scratched eagerly at the gate.

Nanny looked up. "Why, hello, little pup," she said as Lucky wagged his tail. "Too bad you can't come with us. But you're not a Dalmatian. You should go find your own family—I'm sure they're worried about you."

Lucky was confused, but then he caught sight of his reflection in a nearby puddle. He was covered with dirt. He looked like a Labrador puppy—Nanny didn't recognize him!

Lucky realized he had to wash the mud off his fur right away. He ran to join some children who were playing in a fountain.

The children giggled as the little Dalmatian jumped about in the fountain, then shook himself clean.

A man sitting on a nearby bench looked over and frowned. He was not happy. His newspaper was covered with water and mud.

Lucky ran toward home. He grinned as he spotted Nanny crouching in front of the house, unhooking his brothers' and sisters' leashes.

"My goodness," she said as Lucky ran past her and into the house. "Where did you come from?"

Later, when Pongo and Perdita came home, they found Lucky curled up in the sleeping basket.

"You see?" Pongo whispered to Perdita. "I told you nothing would go wrong."

THE
LION KING
A Day Without Pumbaa

"Mmm!" said Timon. "Breakfast time! Come to daddy, you tasty little critters."

Timon was showing Simba how to catch the plentiful but sneaky bugs that crept and flew throughout the jungle.

"Too bad Pumbaa has to miss out on this feast," Timon said. "I haven't seen him since sunup. Have you? Ooh! There's a good one! Quiet now. . . . Watch me, Simba . . . and learn!"

Timon crouched stealthily behind a rotting log crawling with beetles. He was just about to leap, when . . . "AAARGH!"

Without any warning at all, Pumbaa came hurtling out of the treetops, swinging wildly on a vine . . . straight into Timon. In an instant, Timon was a meerkat pancake.

"Oops . . . sorry, Timon," Pumbaa said.

"Sorry!" fumed Timon. "Sorry, you say! That's the nineteenth— no, the twentieth time you've crashed into me this week!"

"But it wasn't on purpose," Pumbaa told him.

"You never do anything on purpose," Timon replied. "You're a natural disaster! Why, you couldn't catch a bug if it flew into your mouth."

"That's not true!" Pumbaa protested. "Look! I'll prove it."

The clumsy warthog lunged for a juicy grub, only to fall headfirst into a mud puddle—splattering Simba and Timon from head to toe.

"That's it!" cried Timon. "I've had it! No more disasters!"

Pumbaa looked heartbroken. "Do you think I'm a disaster, too?" he asked Simba.

"Well . . ." Simba began, "you have to admit, sometimes you do do pretty disastrous things."

Pumbaa hung his head. "You're right," he said. "Nobody wants me around. It'd be better for everyone if I just left." And with that, he plodded off into the jungle.

Just then, the clouds thickened, and a bolt of lightning shot across the sky.

"Wait a second," said Simba. "Timon, we can't let him go!"

But Timon didn't even turn to look. "If that warthog thinks I'm going to beg him to stay, he's sorely mistaken. Trust me, Simba," said Timon, "he'll be back by lunchtime."

But as the rain began to pour down, Simba wasn't so sure.

The storm came and went. And so did lunch . . . and dinner. And still no Pumbaa. Simba began to worry—a lot.

"We shouldn't have been so hard on him," said the cub. "I wonder if he's okay."

"He's fine," snapped Timon, who was still sore from getting squashed that morning. "Besides, he's the one who walked out on us, remember? Poof! Gone! History, as far as I'm concerned. Pumbaa? Who's that? Never heard of him!"

Simba sighed.

"Oh, stop moping," Timon said, "and think about it. We can do anything we want now—without worrying about getting knocked down, covered with mud, or run over. Let's enjoy it."

So off they went. First, they tried chasing vultures. Then, they splashed in the river. They even tried playing a game of tag among the vines. But somehow, nothing they did seemed like very much fun. Something—or someone—was always missing.

"So, what do you want to do now?" Timon asked Simba.

"I don't know," said Simba. "What do you want to do?"

"I asked you first," said Timon.

The sun began to dip below the horizon. Timon sighed. He was bored. And, he admitted to himself, it was also possible that he missed Pumbaa, just a little.

"There's got to be something fun to do," said Simba.

"Well," said Timon gloomily, "what do you want to do?"

"I don't know," said Simba. "What do you want to do?"

And so they went on . . . and on . . . and on. And they would have gone on even longer, if a sudden rustling along the riverbank hadn't interrupted them.

"Timon! Simba! Look what I found!"

Like a giddy tornado, Pumbaa tumbled out of the jungle, sweeping up Timon and Simba and sending all three of them crashing into the trunk of a large tree. The bugs Pumbaa had brought for his friends went flying into the air and then hit the ground—*Plop*! *Plop*! *Plop*!

"I'm back," Pumbaa groaned.

"So we see," mumbled Timon.

Miserably, Pumbaa stood up and faced his crumpled friends. "I came back to say I missed you," he said. "But now look what I've done! I'm the worst friend ever."

"Now, wait one minute!" cried Timon. "That's just not true!"

"You're a wonderful friend, and we miss you!" said Simba. "We even miss your disasters."

"It appears," said Timon wryly, "that we've grown accustomed to being stepped on, bruised, and squashed."

"You mean you're willing to put up with me?" asked Pumbaa, trying to hold back his happy tears.

"You bet!" said Simba. "You're our very favorite disaster."

Aladdin

Abu's Adventure

The Magic Carpet swooped through the Agrabah marketplace.

"Abu! Stop covering my eyes!" Aladdin cried as he tried to pry the monkey's arms from around his head. "How can I find a gift for the Genie when I can't see?"

Abu didn't let go. The Magic Carpet was speeding between the stalls. Suddenly, the Carpet stopped short. Aladdin disentangled himself from Abu's grip as he hopped off the Carpet.

"Thanks, Carpet." Aladdin gave the rug a high five on one of its tassels.

Abu followed Aladdin and the Carpet to a stall that was packed with interesting things. Although they had been to the marketplace a hundred times, none of them had ever seen this stall before.

"May I help you?" asked the merchant in the stall. He was tall and very thin, and his eyes were a strange yellow color.

"What's this?" Aladdin asked as he picked up an unusual blue tube.

"Hold it to the light, and you will see the colors of the rainbow," the merchant replied.

As the merchant talked to Aladdin, Abu climbed up the side of the stall. Wrapping his tail around a pole, Abu lowered himself so that he was directly above Aladdin.

Then he plucked off Aladdin's hat and put it on his own head. Some people nearby laughed and threw fruit to Abu. Still suspended from the bar, Abu juggled three apples.

"What a clever little monkey you have," the merchant said to Aladdin.

Aladdin turned to look at Abu.

"Give that back!" he cried, snatching his hat from Abu. "Sometimes he's a little too clever," he said to the merchant.

"Perhaps I could buy him from you?" the merchant said. "I also run a troupe of traveling acrobats."

"Sorry," Aladdin replied. "This monkey may be trouble, but he's not for sale."

"I understand," the merchant said.

Although the merchant had many wonderful things on display, none of his wares seemed quite right for the Genie, so Aladdin turned to look at another stall.

The Carpet followed him.

Aladdin searched stand after stand, with no luck. Finally, Aladdin held up an oversize yellow robe. "What do you think of this?" he asked, turning to show it to Abu. "I think the yellow—" Aladdin stopped midsentence.

"Abu?" Aladdin called. He looked around, but there was no sign of Abu. Oh, no, Aladdin said to himself. Abu is angry because I yelled at him. Now he's run away. Come on, Carpet!

Aladdin and the Magic Carpet flew through the marketplace in search of their friend.

"Abu, where are you?" Aladdin cried. But there was no response.

Abu had disappeared!

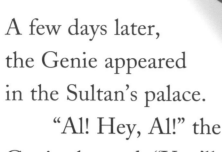

A few days later,
the Genie appeared
in the Sultan's palace.

"Al! Hey, Al!" the
Genie shouted. "You'll never
believe what
I saw!" Suddenly, he noticed Aladdin's
expression. "Hey, why the long face?" he asked.

Aladdin sighed. "I yelled at Abu, and
he ran away."

"Ran away?" The Genie scratched his head. "That's funny,
because I went to see this troupe of acrobats," he said.
"They had a monkey that looked just like Abu! The monkey
flipped through the air, then hung by his tail from a high wire
and juggled four apples."

Aladdin frowned. He was
becoming very uneasy. "You said he looked just
like Abu?" he asked.

The Genie nodded. "He could
have been Abu's twin!"

Suddenly, Aladdin
remembered something that
the man in the marketplace
had said to him just before
Abu disappeared—"I also run a
troupe of traveling acrobats."

"That was no twin!" Aladdin cried, grabbing the Genie by the shoulders. "Genie, Abu didn't run away—he's been monkey-napped! And we've got to save him!"

Meanwhile, Abu sat huddled in a cage. "It's showtime!" Abu heard a low voice say. He turned around and saw two yellow eyes looking in at him. It was the merchant.

Abu tried to crawl into a corner, remembering how the merchant had shoved him into a sack when Aladdin turned his back in the marketplace. But the merchant was too quick. He grabbed Abu and perched him on his shoulder.

"Now, you'll perform like the clever little monkey you are, won't you?" the merchant asked.

Abu stuck out his tongue at the evil merchant.

The merchant frowned. "You'll do it, or there will be no dinner for you tonight!"

Abu sighed. He just had to find a way to escape!

The Genie and Aladdin flew high over the desert on the Magic Carpet.

They had already been to the town where the Genie had seen Abu, but the acrobats had moved on. Nobody knew where they had gone.

"There!" the Genie cried at last.

Aladdin looked down and saw a bright red tent set up in the middle of an oasis. The acrobats were performing in there!

"To the red tent, Carpet," Aladdin said.

The Magic Carpet swooped down toward the oasis.

Aladdin, the Genie, and the Magic Carpet took their seats inside the tent.

After a moment, the lights went down. Then Abu appeared—perched on the high wire!

Aladdin gasped. "Abu!" he shouted. "Be careful!"

The crowd turned to look at Aladdin. "Seize him!" cried the merchant.

As two guards ran toward Aladdin, he and the Genie hopped onto the

Magic Carpet and zoomed toward Abu.

"Grab the monkey!" the merchant shouted, and two of the acrobats began inching out onto the high wire toward Abu.

For a moment, Abu stood in the middle of the high wire, not moving. He knew that if the acrobats caught him, he'd have to go back to his cage.

Finally, Abu made a decision. He closed his eyes and jumped.

"Gotcha!" Aladdin cried as Abu landed safely in his arms. The audience cheered. Aladdin had forgotten that he was in the middle of a crowd, but Abu knew just what to do. He waved, then stuck out his tongue at the angry merchant as he flew away with his friends, free at last.

Ariel and the Sea-Horse Race

King Triton, ruler of all the oceans, stormed through the palace courtyard.

"Ariel!" His voice thundered.

The young mermaid appeared, riding her sea horse, Stormy.

"Daddy, I know what you are going to say—" Ariel began, but King Triton interrupted his daughter, waving a scroll angrily.

"Ariel, how could you sign up for the Annual Sea-Horse Race?" he asked. "It's a dangerous competition! No mermaid has ever competed in this race."

Ariel raised her chin defiantly. "Mermaids ride sea horses, too, Daddy," she said. "And Stormy may be small, but he's fast. I know we can win that race if you'll only give us a chance."

"You take too many chances!" King Triton shouted.

"But, Daddy . . ." Ariel pleaded.

"No, Ariel. I forbid you to enter the race!" he said.

Ariel knew there was no point in arguing with her

father anymore. With tears in her eyes, she and Stormy slowly made their way out of the palace courtyard.

Ariel moped around the racecourse all week long. Her best friend, Flounder, tried to cheer her up.

"That old sea-horse trophy isn't so great, anyway," said Flounder. "Why don't we go exploring for human stuff?"

But for once, Ariel didn't want to look for human treasures. She only had one thing on her mind.

"It just isn't fair!" she exclaimed. "I know I could win!"

"Yes," agreed Flounder. "If you were a merman, your father would let you sign up."

"That's it!" cried Ariel. "I'll be a merman—Arrol, the merman! Flounder, you're a genius!"

Ariel swam around the palace, looking for a racing uniform and helmet. As she turned a corner, she swam smack into her father's adviser, Sebastian the crab.

"Teenagers," muttered Sebastian. "Always in a hurry."

"Sorry, Sebastian," said Ariel. "I guess I just had racing on my mind."

"You and your father both," Sebastian said as he adjusted his shell. "He keeps going to the closet to look at his old racing uniform. You know, he was just your age when he entered his first competition."

Ariel was surprised. King Triton had never told her that he used to race.

"Thanks, Sebastian!" said Ariel. Now she knew just where to find a racing uniform!

On the morning of the competition, Ariel hid with Stormy near the starting line, her tail swishing back and forth nervously.

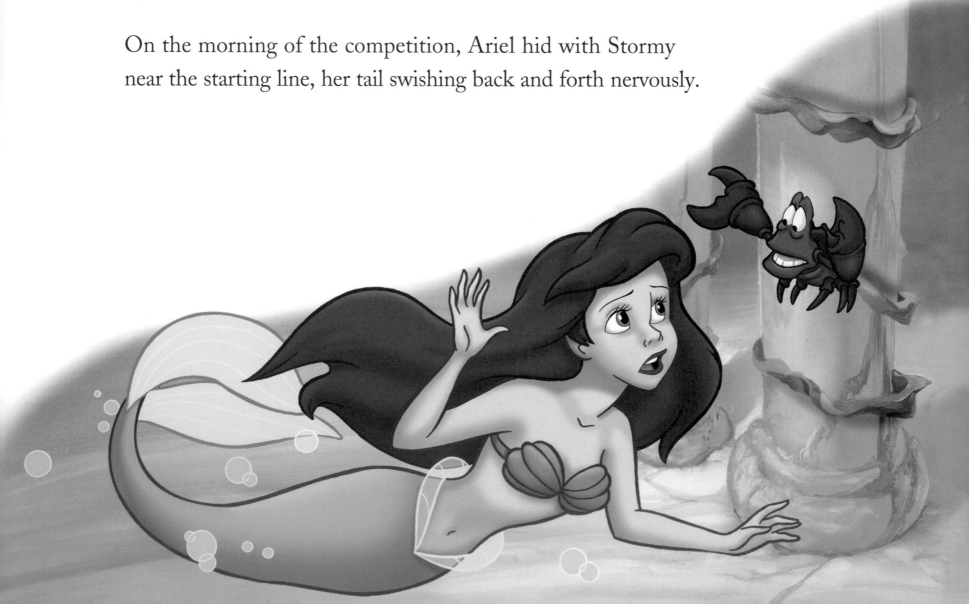

Just then, the trumpets sounded. King Triton raised his trident. Quickly, Ariel swung herself onto Stormy's back and urged the sea horse to the starting line, where they joined the other contestants.

A spark shot out of the tip of Triton's trident. The racers steered their sea horses through the water at breakneck speed. When they reached the coral reef, many of the fastest and more powerful sea horses could not fit through the small openings and had to swim around the coral reef.

But Stormy was small and Ariel was brave. They zipped in and out of the spiky coral. It was not long before they had taken the lead.

"YAHOO!" Ariel shouted with joy. Her cry gave Stormy a burst of energy. The sea horse whipped around the next turn. But this time he was

too fast! Ariel's helmet hit the coral and popped off. Her long red hair streamed out behind her.

Ariel's heart was pounding with excitement and fear. Behind her, the mermen were gaining speed.

One racer, Carpa, saw Ariel before she dove into the dark cavern. "A mermaid!" he roared, and urged his powerful sea horse to top speed.

It was pitch-black in the cavern, but Ariel and Stormy knew the way. They had been there before, searching for treasures.

Suddenly, Ariel and Stormy were pushed roughly from behind. Ariel clung tightly to Stormy, but they were pushed again.

"What was that?" Ariel cried, as she pulled Stormy back on course.

She turned around. It was Carpa!

Stormy was frightened. He raced ahead and swam out of the cavern at record speed. He headed for the last part of the racecourse: the seaweed hurdles.

Ariel and Stormy swam over and under the seaweed hurdles. All of Atlantica could see them now. The crowd gasped as everyone recognized King Triton's youngest daughter. The Sea King rose from the royal box, a look of utter surprise on his regal face.

"You haven't won yet, mermaid!" came a rough voice behind Ariel, as Carpa pulled up beside her.

"Neither have you!" Ariel cried, urging Stormy on.

With one last burst of speed, Stormy raced across the finish line.

"Hooray!" cried Ariel's sisters. Flounder did flips as the spectators roared their approval.

Ariel smiled broadly and waved. Then she caught sight of her father. He was looking at her sternly.

Nervously, Ariel steered Stormy toward the royal box. There stood King Triton, holding a gleaming trophy.

"Daddy, I . . ." Ariel began, but she never finished her sentence because King Triton had enveloped her in a giant hug.

"Oh, Ariel, I'm sorry I was so unreasonable," he said. "I had forgotten how much fun racing could be. All I thought about was how dangerous it was for you to be in a competition like this one. Will you ever forgive your stubborn father?"

Ariel nodded and kissed his rough cheek. Then, proudly, King Triton handed his daughter—the first mermaid ever to win the Annual Sea-Horse Race—her trophy.

A Tight Squeeze

"Okay," Woody called to all the toys in Andy's room. "The coast is clear."

It was early one morning, and Andy had just left for school. He would be gone all day, and the toys had the room to themselves.

"So, Woody," said Rex as the toys gathered in the center of the floor, "what's this game you were telling us about?"

Woody smiled. "It's called sardines," he replied. "It's like hide-and-seek, except the toy who's 'It' is the one who hides, and everyone else tries to find him or her."

Buzz scratched his head. "Well, what do you do when you find the hider?" he asked Woody.

"Oh, yeah," said Woody. "That's the fun part. When you find the hider, you also hide with them and wait for someone else to find you both. Then, the next toy to find you hides with you, too, and so on and so on. Get it?"

Most of the toys smiled and nodded at Woody. Bo Peep clapped her hands. "Ooh, this is going to be fun!" she cried.

But Jessie was still confused about one thing. "So, by the end of the game, everyone is hiding together in one spot?" she asked.

Woody nodded. "Right," he said, "except for the last toy who is still looking for the hiders. In the next game, that toy is 'It'—the one who hides!"

Now all the toys understood the rules and were ready to play!

"So let's decide who's 'It,'" Woody suggested. "I'm thinking of a number between one and one hundred. Whoever guesses closest to that number is 'It.'"

The toys took turns guessing. Woody was thinking of forty-nine. Hamm guessed forty-seven. He was the closest, so he was "It."

"Okay, everybody," Woody announced. "Close your eyes and count to twenty-five while Hamm hides."

The toys closed their eyes and began to count aloud: "One . . . two . . . three . . ."

Meanwhile, Hamm hurried away and started looking for a good hiding place. "Hmm . . ." he said to himself as he considered hiding inside Andy's toy chest. "Nah, too obvious. That's the first place they'd look."

"Ten . . . eleven . . . twelve . . ." the toys continued counting.

Hamm hurried over to Andy's bed and peeked under the dust ruffle. It was dark and dusty under the bed. "Nah," said Hamm. "Too scary. I'm not hiding under there all by myself."

"Eighteen . . . nineteen . . . twenty . . ." the
toys counted off.

Hamm was running out of time! With only
seconds to spare, he spotted one of Andy's old
lunch boxes, raced over to it, hopped inside,
and closed the lid.

"Whew!" he whispered to himself. "That was close, but I'm hidden!" Only then
did Hamm realize that it was even darker inside the closed lunch box than it was
under Andy's bed. "Huh," said Hamm, feeling slightly panicked but trying to keep
his cool. "I, uh, wonder how long it'll take for someone to find me."

To his great relief, just one minute later, the lunch-box lid was lifted open and
a Green Army Man peeked in. Upon spotting Hamm, he waved his battalion in.
"Target located. Move, move, move!" he ordered as more Green Army Men scaled
the side of the lunch box and rappelled down to Hamm's side.

Within seconds, they were all in and the lid was closed again.

"Hey, guys," Hamm said, glad to have company.
"What took you so long?"

The next toy to open the lunch-box lid was Woody, whose eyes lit up when he saw Hamm and the Green Army Men inside. He glanced over his shoulder to make sure he wasn't being watched before he hopped inside the lunch box to join the hiders.

As soon as Woody was in and the lid was closed, he noticed that Hamm was standing very close to him. "Uh, Hamm," Woody said, "could you scooch over a little? I'm feeling a bit cramped."

"Gee, Woody," Hamm replied. "I'd like to help you out, but I'm already squished up against the sergeant, here." He pointed to the Green Army Man on the other side of him.

"Hmm . . ." said Woody. "This may become a problem."

Just then, the lid opened and Jessie peeked in. "Yippee!" she cried as she hopped inside the lunch box. "Found ya, didn't I?"

But there was no free floor space left inside the lunch box. Jessie got wedged between Hamm and Woody.

"Well, gosh, boys," said Jessie. "It's a little bit crowded in here, isn't it?"

The situation only got worse as more and more toys found the hiders.

Slinky Dog only managed to fit inside by standing over a Green Army Man.

"Ow, your paw is in my ear," the Green Army Man told Slinky Dog.

Buzz heard the toys complaining and located the hiding place. "Make way, folks!" he exclaimed as he piled in. But as hard as he tried, he couldn't get the lid to close.

By the time Rex found the hiders, there was absolutely no way he could even climb in.

"Hey, no fair!" Rex exclaimed. "I found you guys, but there's no room for me to hide with you. What do I do now, Woody?"

"Shhhh!" Woody said, raising a finger to his lips. "Keep your voice down or everyone will come over and see where we're hiding."

But it was too late. The rest of the toys were already hurrying over to the overstuffed lunch box.

"Oh, well," said Woody with a laugh. "Everyone has found us, so this game is over. Everybody out!"

One by one, the toys tumbled out of the lunch box and gathered around Hamm. "Gosh, Hamm, couldn't you have picked a bigger hiding place?" Rex asked him.

Hamm's cheeks blushed as all the toys waited for an answer. Then, thinking quickly, Hamm replied, "Well, yeah, but isn't the point of the game to get squished? Like sardines in a can? The game is called sardines, isn't it?"

The toys thought that over and had to agree. "You've got a point there, Hamm," said Buzz.

And from then on, every time the toys played sardines, the hider made sure to pick a small hiding place—just to keep things interesting!

Who's in Charge?

"Now, Dory," said Marlin, "are you sure you can handle watching Nemo for a little while this afternoon? I just have a few errands to run, and I'll only be gone a couple of hours. But you have to promise you'll keep a close eye on him. Can you do that?"

Outside Marlin and Nemo's anemone home, Marlin darted this way and that, "pacing" anxiously, while Dory and Nemo calmly looked on.

"I can do that!" Dory replied confidently.

"We'll be fine, Dad," Nemo said. "Don't worry."

But Marlin was a little worried. It was a simple fact that Dory forgot things—often, important things. And there were three things that Nemo needed to get done that afternoon.

"Now remember, both of you," Marlin instructed them, "while I'm gone, Nemo needs to do his science homework, practice playing his conch shell, and clean the anemone. Okay, say that back to me."

"Nemo needs to . . . um . . . oh, it's right at the tip of my tongue," Dory said.

"Science homework, conch shell, clean the anemone," said Nemo. "I got it, Dad. No problem."

"That's right! What he said," Dory agreed.

Finally, Marlin waved good-bye and swam off to do his errands.

As soon as he was gone, Dory began swimming in circles around the anemone.

"Hee, hee, hee!" she laughed as she raced around and around. "Nemo, betcha can't catch me! No way! 'Cause you're too slow. . . ."

Nemo raced off, chasing Dory around the anemone a few times. It was fun, and Nemo wished they could play all afternoon. But he knew they couldn't. So he stopped chasing Dory and tried to get her attention.

"Dory, come on," Nemo called to her. "That was fun, but now I'd better get started on my science homework."

Dory swam over. "Your science homework?" she said as she tried to catch her breath. "Aw, can't you do that tomorrow?"

Nemo shook his head. "Like my dad said, I have to do it this afternoon," he explained. "It's due tomorrow."

Nemo explained his assignment to Dory: he had to find a sand dollar to bring into class the next day.

So Nemo and Dory swam around the reef, looking for a sand dollar. Before long, Nemo spotted one lying on the seafloor under a coral outcropping. He picked it up gently.

"I found one!" Nemo exclaimed.

"That's great!" replied Dory. "Now we can play!"

But Nemo reminded her about their to-do list. "No, Dory," he said. "Now I need to practice playing my conch shell."

"You do?" said Dory, sounding disappointed.

Nemo sighed. "Didn't you hear my dad say that?" he asked. "I have band practice tomorrow at school."

"Oh," Dory said with a shrug. "That's news to me, but all right."

They swam back to the anemone, where Nemo put his sand dollar away and got out his conch shell. He had Dory keep time while he played the songs that he needed to memorize for band practice.

"Yeah, play it, Nico!" Dory exclaimed as she grooved to the tunes.

Nemo played and played and played until he felt ready for band practice the next day.

"Thanks, Dory!" he said at last. "We're done."

"Yippee!" Dory shouted, swimming excitedly around Nemo. "Now it's playtime!"

But Nemo remembered their work wasn't done yet. "Not quite, Dory," he said. "I have to clean the anemone before I can play."

"Clean?" Dory said with a frustrated sigh. "On a beautiful afternoon like this?"

Nemo shrugged. "Dad said I should do it before he got home," he replied.

Together, Dory and Nemo cleaned up the zooplankton crumbs that were cluttering the anemone. It only took a few minutes, but when they were finished, the place was spotless.

"Thanks for helping me, Dory," said Nemo. "That went fast with the two of us working together."

"You're welcome," Dory replied. "So, what do you want to do now?"

Nemo laughed. "What do I want to do now?" he echoed. "I want to play!"

"Play, huh?" Dory said, weighing the idea as if it had never crossed her mind. "Now, that's a crazy idea. I like it!"

So Nemo and Dory played tag. Now and then, Dory forgot who was "It" and wound up getting tagged while she stopped to think. Even so, they had a lot of fun chasing each other until Marlin got home.

"Hi, Dad!" Nemo greeted him.

"Hey, Nemo!" Marlin replied. "Hi, Dory. How was your afternoon?"

"Great!" Dory cried.

"Yeah, great!" Nemo agreed. "I did my science homework, practiced my conch shell, and cleaned the anemone. And we even had time to play!"

Marlin looked impressed. "Wow," he said. Then he turned to Dory. "Good job, Dory. Thanks for watching Nemo and making sure he got everything done. I really appreciate it."

"Aw, don't mention it," Dory replied humbly.

Nemo couldn't believe it! All afternoon, all Dory had wanted to do was play. It was Nemo who had reminded her about the things he needed to get done. And now his dad was giving Dory all the credit?

"But, Dad . . ." Nemo started to object.

Marlin looked over at Nemo and gave him a knowing wink—and Nemo understood. His dad did know the truth, and he was very proud of Nemo.

And that was all the credit Nemo needed.

"Yeah, Dory," said Nemo, patting her on the back. "You're good at being in charge."

The Show Must Go On!

"Flik, long time no see!" cried Rosie the spider as she gave her old friend a hug. "And, Dot," she said, turning to the pint-size ant princess. "You must've grown a whole millimeter since last season!"

The ants had not seen their circus friends since last fall when, with the circus bugs' help, the ants had defeated Hopper, the grasshopper bully who had threatened the colony. Then the circus bugs had gone on tour with P.T. Flea's World's Greatest Circus. But they had promised to visit the colony the following season, and now here they were at last: Rosie, Slim the walking stick, Francis the male ladybug, Heimlich the butterfly, Manny the praying mantis and his moth assistant Gypsy, Dim the beetle, and Tuck and Roll the pill bugs! Even P.T. Flea, the circus owner himself, was there!

"Listen!" Flik said to the circus bugs once he had greeted them all. "Dot and I have a surprise for you. We've organized a variety show with a number of great acts!"

"Yeah," said Dot. "We figured that, as circus performers, you're always entertaining others. So today, we're going to entertain you!"

The circus bugs exchanged excited looks. Gypsy clapped her hands in delight. Heimlich flapped his tiny butterfly wings. Francis good-naturedly elbowed Slim in the side.

"Ouch!" cried Slim.

"Oops! Sorry, Slim," Francis replied. "So, Flik, when's curtain time?"

"Right away!" exclaimed Flik. He turned to Dot. "You gather the performers," he told her. "I'll organize the audience. Deal?"

"Deal!" Dot replied. She hurried off in the direction of the anthill while Flik led the circus bugs, along with a crowd of ant onlookers, over toward a makeshift stage he and Dot had constructed in the middle of a clearing.

Minutes later, Flik took his place onstage as the variety-show emcee. He had seated the circus bugs front and center, and the ants had filled in around them, also eager to watch the performances. Now all they needed were the performers.

Just then, Flik spotted Dot hurrying toward him with the stars of the show in tow: Queen Atta and her mother, a dozen or so ants from Dot's Blueberry troop, and three ant boys named Reed, Grub, and Jordy. Flik cleared his throat and began his introduction of the first act.

"Okay, everybody," Flik announced, "welcome to the first-ever ant-colony variety show! Today's performance is dedicated to our special guests, the circus bugs!"

The audience clapped and cheered.

"Now, sit back, relax, and enjoy the musical stylings of Queen Atta and Princess Dot, singing 'High Hopes.' Come on, folks, let's give 'em a big hand!"

Flik clapped with the audience as he waited for Dot and Atta to take the stage. But when the performers did not appear, Flik rushed offstage to find Dot and Atta looking very anxious. "What's the matter?" he whispered to them.

Atta opened her mouth to reply, but no words came out.

"Atta's lost her voice," Dot explained. "She can't sing. We can't do our number."

Flik was flustered for a moment, but quickly regained his composure. "Okay, okay," he said. "We'll just move on to the second act."

Dot looked worriedly at Atta.

"What?" said Flik. "There's a problem with the second act?"

"Aphie has stage fright," Dot replied. Flik looked over at the Queen Mother and her trembling pet, Aphie, and saw that the second act was a lost cause, too.

"Third act?" Flik asked Dot hopefully.

Dot shook her head. "The captain of the Blueberry acrobatic team isn't here yet," she explained. "Without her, there's no one to top their pyramid."

Flik looked questioningly at Reed, Grub, and Jordy. "What about you, boys?" he asked them. "Ready to go on? Those jokes of yours will leave them rolling in the aisles!"

But the boys were hesitant. "We can't go out there first," said Reed.

"That crowd is not even warmed up," added Grub.

Flik sighed and dropped his head, feeling utterly defeated. "Well, that's our whole show, down the drain," he said with a shrug. "I guess I'll just have to go out there and tell them that our first-ever ant-colony variety show is over . . . before it even began."

Flik turned to walk onstage, but found his way blocked—by the circus bugs!

"The crowd is getting restless," Francis said.

"Anything we can do to help?" Rosie asked gently.

Reluctantly, Flik explained the situation to his guests of honor. "Atta can't sing, Aphie has stage fright, the Blueberry acrobatic team captain didn't show, and our comedy act here won't go on without a warmed-up crowd."

The circus bugs just smiled. They were used to improvising when things didn't go as planned.

"The show must go on!" P.T. Flea exclaimed.

"Right!" cried Rosie. "Now, here's what we're going to do." The circus bugs pulled Flik and Dot into a huddle, and they made their game plan.

Then, lo and behold, the show did go on!

The first act delighted the crowd with the sweet sounds of Dot and Rosie, who, as it happened, knew all the words to "High Hopes."

The second act had the audience in stitches as Dim played the role of Aphie the aphid in the Queen Mother's amazing aphid act.

The third act wowed the spectators with the balance and agility of the Blueberry acrobatic team, who took on two honorary members, Tuck and Roll.

By the fourth act, the crowd was sufficiently warmed up, and Reed, Grub, and Jordy took the stage to amuse the audience with their best jokes.

Then, as the first-ever ant-colony variety show came to a close, all the performers took a bow before a cheering crowd. Flik and Dot looked up and down the row of performers, and into the wings at the other circus bugs clapping for them, and they smiled. So the show hadn't turned out exactly the way they had planned it. But working together with the circus bugs toward a common goal—whether it was defeating grasshopper bullies or putting on a variety show—was just like old times. And that felt great!

DISNEY·PIXAR
MONSTERS, INC.

The Last Laugh

Ever since Monsters, Inc. had made the changeover from collecting scream energy to collecting laugh energy from human children, Mike Wazowski had gotten used to his reputation as the funniest monster in the company and status as number one in the laugh-collecting department.

"Feeling funny today?" Sulley asked Mike on the Laugh Floor one morning. Sulley was the president of Monsters, Inc. and Mike's best friend.

Mike smiled. "You bet! You wanna hear some of my new material? So this monster walks into a deli—"

Just then, a chorus of hysterical laughter filled the Laugh Floor, catching Mike off guard.

"Hey," said Mike, looking around to see where the laughter was coming from, "if you think that's good, wait till you hear the punch line!"

But Mike quickly realized the laughter wasn't for him. Across the Laugh Floor, a group of employees stood guffawing around another monster. Mike turned to Sulley. "Who's the comedian?" he asked.

"You haven't met Stan, our newest recruit?" Sulley replied, looking surprised. "Come on. I'll introduce you."

Sulley led Mike across the room toward the group of employees.

"Good morning, Mr. Sullivan!" Stan said when he saw Sulley approaching.

Sulley extended a hand in greeting. "Please, Stan, call me Sulley," he replied. "Hey, there's someone I'd like you to meet." Sulley turned to Mike, who was standing at his side. "Mike Wazowski, this is Stanley Stanford. Stan just joined our laugh team yesterday," Sulley said to Mike. Then he turned to Stan. "Mike here is our top Laugh Collector. He has been with us since we started collecting laugh energy," Sulley explained. "And long before that, too."

Mike and Stan shook hands as one of the can wranglers, Needleman, tapped Stan on the shoulder. "Mr. Stanford," he said eagerly, "tell them the joke you just told us." Needleman turned to Mike. "You've just gotta hear this one, Mr. Wazowski."

Stan seemed reluctant at first, so Mike encouraged him.

"Come on, Stan," said Mike, "let's hear it. I love a good laugh."

"Well, all right," Stan replied with a shrug. "I was just telling them about the time I met the Abominable Snowman and his mother. I said to him, 'Hey, Mr. Snowman, where's your mother from?' And he said, 'Alaska.' And I said, 'Hey, don't bother. I'll ask her myself!'"

All the employees burst out laughing all over again—everyone except Mike, who couldn't help feeling just a tiny bit green with envy. Who did this guy think he was, Mike thought, waltzing in there and stealing all the laughs, when it was he, Mike Wazowski, who had been there for so long, honing his craft, working hard for every giggle, guffaw, and chuckle?

Mike felt like his reputation as the number one laugh-getter at Monsters, Inc. was being challenged! He had to step up and remind everyone who was king—king of laughs—before they all decided that Stan was funnier than he was!

"Hey, good one, Stan," Mike said when the laughter had died down. "But have you heard the one about the skeleton who decided not to go to the party?" All eyes turned to Mike as the crowd waited for the punch line: "He had no *body* to go with!" Mike exclaimed.

A wave of laughter crashed over Mike. He was back on top!

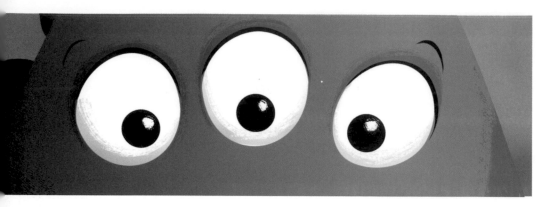

But Stan had another joke. "That's funny, Mike," he said. "Have you heard the one about the big elephant that wouldn't stop charging? The only way to stop him was to take away his credit card!"

Now everyone was laughing at Stan again. Mike's eye narrowed in determination as he called all of his best jokes to mind. No one could beat him in a joke showdown!

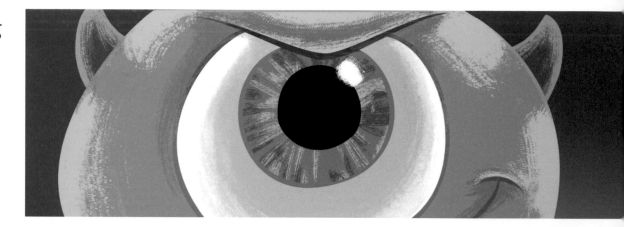

As the jokes came fast and furious, the employees formed a circle around the two jokesters.

"Did you hear the story about the oatmeal?" Mike said. "Aw, never mind. It was a lot of mush!"

"What do you call a chicken at the North Pole?" Stan said, posing a riddle. "Lost!"

"Anybody know the difference between a dancer and a duck?" Mike called out. "One dances Swan Lake, the other swims in it!"

"What is a monster's favorite play?" Stan asked the crowd. "Romeo and Ghouliet!"

Pretty soon, the crowd of employees was laughing so hard and so loud that they could barely hear the jokes. Yet the joke-off continued until—in a moment of panic—Mike completely blanked on all of his jokes! The harder he tried to think of a joke, the emptier his mind became! What would he do? What would he say? It was his turn, and the employees' laughter began to die down as they awaited Mike's next joke. As his anxiety grew, Mike began to jump up and down, hoping to jump-start his brain, but nothing was coming to him.

Then, in one of his panicky little jumps, Mike accidentally landed on the edge of a four-wheeled dolly that the employees used to move heavy things around the Laugh Floor.

"Waaaaaaah!" Mike cried as the dolly took off, rolling across the room and carrying him with it, completely off balance and out of control.

The employees watched as Mike careened wildly across the Laugh Floor. They fell down, paralyzed by laughter. When Mike landed in a pile of empty cardboard boxes, the joke-off was officially over, and Mike was the hands-down winner.

Sulley and Stan helped Mike out of the pile of boxes.

"You're a funny guy, Mike Wazowski," Stan said, giving Mike a pat on the back.

Mike smiled. Stan wasn't such a bad guy, after all. And with two hilarious monsters on the laugh team, thought Mike, just imagine all the laugh energy they could collect!

Still, Mike didn't want to let on that his dramatic exit had been an accident. So he put his arm around Stan's shoulders and offered him a piece of advice.

"If there's one thing I've learned over the years," said Mike, "it's never underestimate the power of slapstick."

DISNEY PRESENTS A **PIXAR** FILM

THE INCREDIBLES

Super Annoying!

Dash was bored. It was Saturday afternoon, and he had run out of things to do. He had already taken a twenty-mile run, cooled off with fifty laps over at the town pool, and chased the neighbor's dog around the block. But with Dash's Super speed, that had only killed about five minutes.

He was sitting in his messy bedroom on his unmade bed, wondering what to do, when his mother, Helen, walked past the doorway.

"You know, Dash," his mom said, stopping to poke her head into the room, "if you're looking for something to do, you could clean up your . . ." Before Helen had a chance to finish, Dash raced around his room and cleaned it up.

"I'm still bored," Dash said with a groan.

"Well, you could . . . read a book," Helen said as she left his room.

That's boring, thought Dash.

Just then, the telephone rang. Violet raced out of her bedroom to get it, and Dash's eyes zeroed in on her. Target spotted.

Now this will be fun, he said to himself. Dash stopped in Violet's doorway. A sly grin slowly spread across his face.

Dash's eyes darted back and forth between Violet's bedroom and the kitchen, making sure his sister wasn't looking. Then he hurried into her room in search of a good place to hide.

Five minutes later, Violet came back into her room and closed the door behind her. She started to cross to her bed, but halfway there she stopped in her tracks and looked around. Things were not as she had left them. The bedspread was upside down. The lampshade on her lamp was missing; her books had been moved around; and the posters that hung around her mirror were rearranged.

"Mom! Dash rearranged all of my stuff!" Violet yelled.

As Helen walked down the hall, a breeze whipped through Violet's room. Helen looked inside.

"It looks fine to me, honey. Your brother is reading a book in his room. Now I've got to get dinner ready," she said.

Violet's eyes scanned the room. Everything was back in place.

Then her eyes fell on the closet door, which stood ajar. She went over to the door and threw it open.

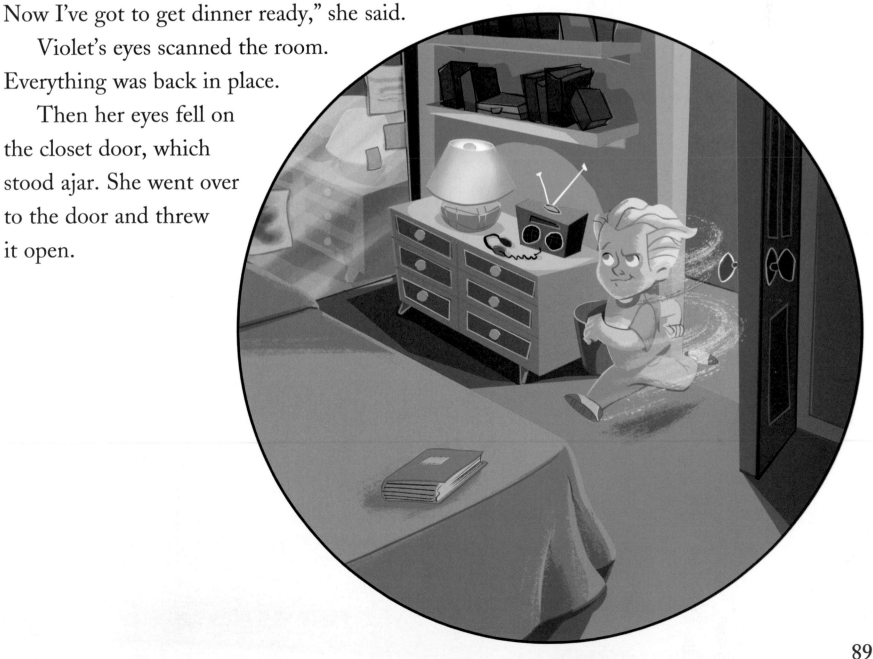

"Dash!" Violet exclaimed, pushing some clothes aside to find her brother crouched behind them. "Get out of here, you little insect!"

Dash jumped up wearing some of Violet's clothes. "Look at me. I'm Violet. I'm in love with Tony Rydinger."

Violet reached in, grabbed Dash by one arm, and pulled him out of the closet. Then she dragged him across the room and pushed him out into the hall.

"Stay out of my room!" Violet yelled, slamming the door behind her brother.

Dash dropped the clothes in the hall, sped out the front door of the house, and snuck around to the backyard. He stood on tiptoe to peer in through Violet's bedroom window. Violet hadn't even had time to cross the room and sit down on her bed before she spotted her little brother staring in at her.

"Yoo-hoo, Violet!" Dash called to her in a sickly-sweet, singsong voice as he threw her a dainty wave.

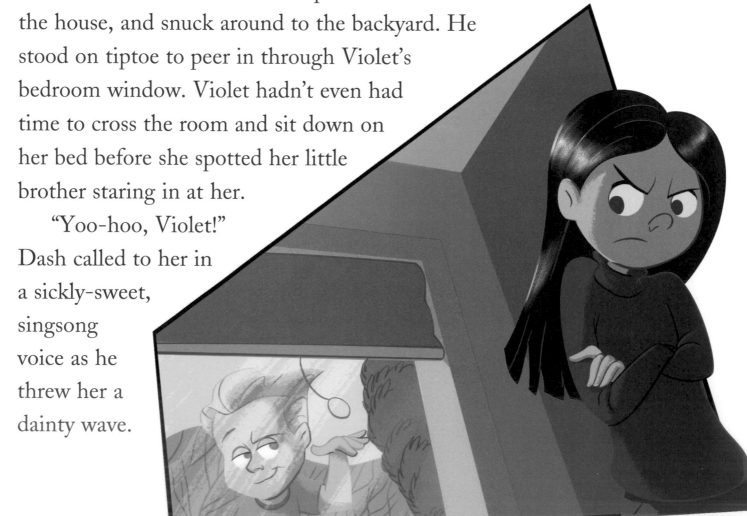

Violet rushed to the window and pulled down the shade.

As she sat on her bed, she felt something under her. "Aaaahhh!" she screamed.

"Forget to lock something?" Dash said, poking his head out from under the covers. Then he zoomed around and around—up onto the bed, down to the floor, around Violet—all at such Super speed that Violet couldn't even tell where he was at any given moment. All she saw was a blur flying around her room, kicking up a whirlwind of papers and blowing pictures off her mirror.

"Dash!" Violet shouted. "Knock it off!"

But Dash only came to a halt when he spotted Violet's diary, which had been blown off a bookshelf and had fallen open on her bed.

"Ooooh," Dash said, picking up the diary and eyeing it excitedly. "What have we here? Oh . . . poetry." Dash continued in a fake English accent. "'I love Tony. He dost the cutest. Shall I compare him to a . . .'"

That was it. Violet had had just about enough of Dash. "Give me that back!" she yelled.

Dash tried to race out of the room, but using her Super power, Violet threw a force field in front of the door. Dash ran into it head on and was knocked to the floor. The diary fell out of his hand, and Violet quickly snatched it away. But before she knew it, the diary flew out of her hand in a sudden wind.

"'How dost I love thee?'" Dash read the diary from the other side of the room.

Violet turned invisible and lunged at Dash. "You are gonna get it!" she cried.

Dash and Violet continued to chase each other around Violet's room in a blur of Super powers. Suddenly, they heard their mom calling to them.

"Violet! Dash!" she cried. "Time for dinner!"

Dash froze. Then, in the blink of an eye, he zipped out through the bedroom door and down the hall to the kitchen table.

"Dash," Helen asked, "did you finish your book?"

Then Violet appeared at the table. Her hair was all frazzled.

"Nah," Dash replied. "I found something better to do."